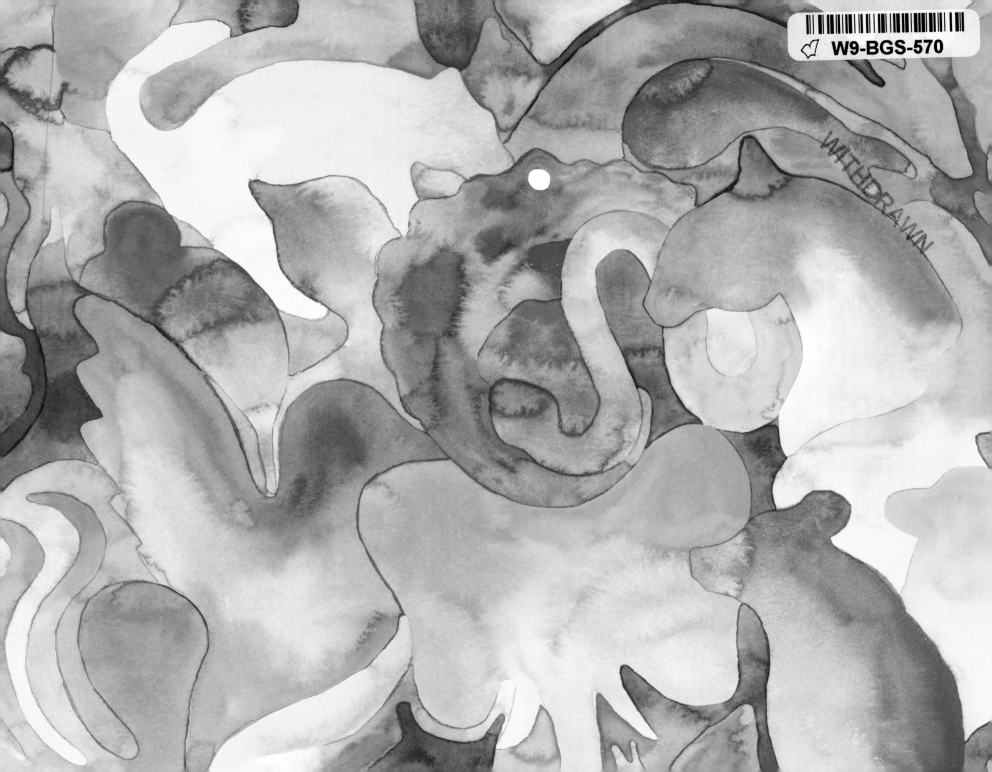

Published by Yeehoo Press
721 W Whittier Blvd, Suite O, La Habra, CA 90631
www.yeehoopress.com

The illustrations for this book were created in watercolor and rendered in photoshop.
This book was designed by Laurel P. Jackson and Hélène Baum-Owoyele.

Library of Congress Control Number: 2021930888
ISBN: 978-1-953458-12-4
Printed in China First Edition
1 2 3 4 5 6 7 8 9 10

the PERFECT PARTY

Written by Laurel P. Jackson

Illustrated by Hélène Baum-Owoyele

YEEHOO PRESS

It was Little Robin's birthday and all the other animals in the zoo wanted to plan the perfect party.

coCoricó.

ohhuu

Mooooooo

cocooooood

Mr. Owl from the United States hollered:
"But we need the perfect fooohhhuuod."

"Oh, yes, and the perfect moosic,"
mooed Mr. Cow from England.

"That's my role, Cocoricó!" Mr. Rooster
from Portugal rushed in and started
to sing, "Cocoricó. Cocoricó."

"No, it's Cockadoodledoo,"
the Jamaican rooster interrupted.

"No, it's Kukurukuu!"
the Nigerian rooster said.

COCKADOODLEDOO COCKADOO

"You all have it wrong.
It is Kikeriki,"
sang the German rooster.

"Stop right there! Wō wō wō,"
yelled the Chinese rooster.

Mr. Goat chimed in,
"my fellow animals, you all know
I have the best voice of all."

He raised his hoof up into the air,
lifted his head and blurted out
the loudest bleat.
"Baaaaaa-aaaaaaa!"

The frogs heard the commotion
and hopped over.

"No. No. No. It is more like this:
Ribbit. Ribbit," sang the Pacific Tree frog.
"Vrak," croaked the Polish frog.
"Kum. Kum," addded the Iranian frog.
"Gae-gool," sang the Korean frog.
"Op. Op," replied the Thai frog.

Each animal tried to out-sing the other more loudly. Little Robin folded his wings over his ears. Soon, all of the animals were screaming, bleating, yapping, and crowing.

They were roaring, mooing, yelping, braying, squawking and meowing until...

SPLAAAAASHHHHH!!!!

Ms. Water Buffalo flung her body into the lake and soaked every single animal. "What a cacophony!" she shouted. "Enough is enough!"

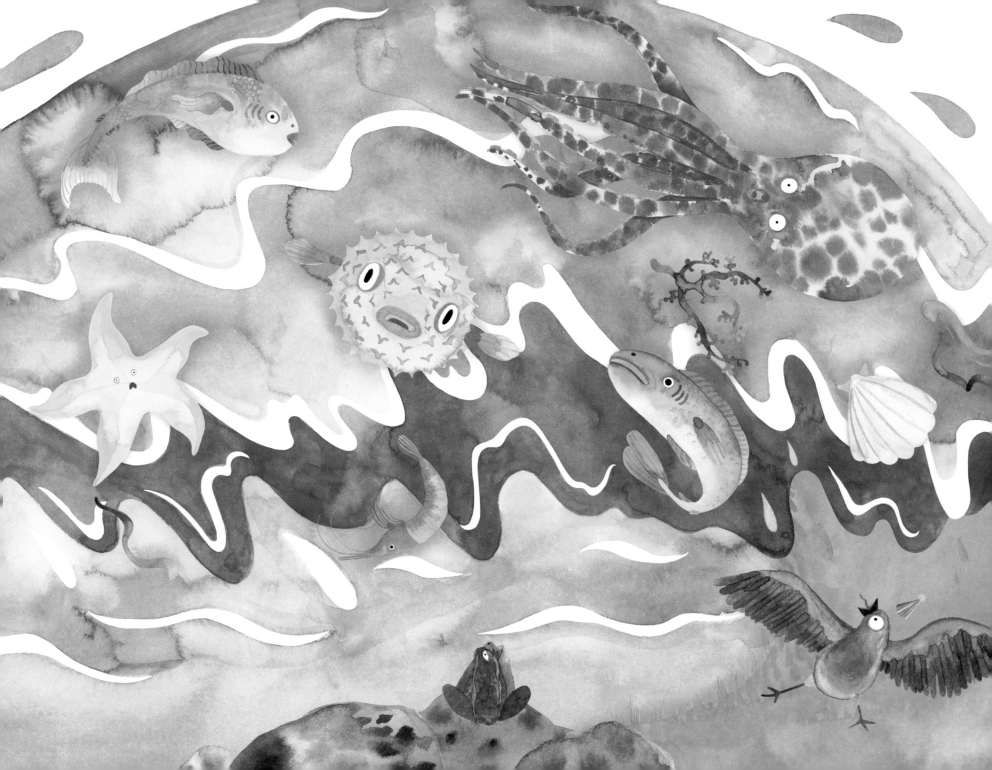

"Ahem, ahem," she cleared her throat.
"Why don't you try singing to-ge-ther?"

"To-ge-ther?" all the animals
responded, confused.

CATS ROOSTERS DOGS BIRDS GOATS FROGS

Ms. Water Buffalo waved her body
to the left.
"Calling all roosters."
She swung her body to the right,
lifted her hands and all the roosters
of the world sang.

"Calling all goats!" She raised her
hands and a large melodious cloud of
sound emerged.

It was marvelous.

Little Robin listened in delight, moving his wings from left to right. All of the animals sang a grand melody. They sang and sang.

"How tweeeeeeet this is. But I am hungry!"
Ms. Parakeet from India shrieked out.

The singing stopped and only
the rumble mumble of tummies
could be heard.

"Hav, hav," barked the Isreali dog! "What about the food?"

"Iii-ahh, iii-ahh," nodded the Spanish donkeys. "Hee, haw, hee haw," agreed the Canadian donkeys.

All of the animals broke out into conversation as they discussed which dish would make the perfect meal.

Mr. Frog from Italy hopped into the forest and collected his ingredients. "Wait until you taste my riiiiiibolita!" "Nothing compares to my cuuuuuuury," replied Ms. Parakeet from India.

All the animals proclaimed their dish to be the best.
And as they prepared their dishes, they argued and bleated,
and yapped, and crowed. They roared, mooed, yelped,
brayed, squawked and meowed until...

KOOR

MIAU

mooousi

eguuusi

iiiiiiiiiiibolita

honk

HAHAHAH

sadzaa

A huge wind came across! It swept up all the dishes, and dumped everything into the small well. No scream, bleat, yap, roar, moo, yelp, bray, squawk or meow was to be heard.

Until...

Little Robin climbed out of the well.
"Heeeeelp me. I fell in," he tweeted.

heeeeelp!!

He was covered from feather to feather and from claw to beak with all of the food.

"Mmmm. Mmmm. Mmmm,"
he licked his feathers.
"This is simply the tastiest thing
I have ever ... mm ... tasted,"
and he flew back in.

All the animals watched in amazement and walked over to the well to have a taste for themselves. It was good. "Mmmmmmm" was the only sound for the rest of the celebration.

And so with the perfect music sung
and the perfect meal prepared,
the animals threw the perfect party
for Little Robin.